The Butterfly Dance

For Sonny, Johnny and Florrie

Bloomsbury Publishing,
London, Oxford, New York, New Delhi and Sydney

First published in Great Britain in 2017 by Bloomsbury Publishing Plc
50 Bedford Square, London WC1B 3DP

This paperback edition first published in 2018

www.bloomsbury.com

BLOOMSBURY is a registered trademark of Bloomsbury Publishing Plc

Text and illustrations copyright © Suzanne Barton 2017

The moral rights of the author/illustrator have been asserted

A CIP catalogue record of this book is available from the British Library

ISBN 978 1 4088 6485 2 (PB)
ISBN 978 1 4088 7384 7 (eBook)

All papers used by Bloomsbury Publishing are natural, recyclable products made from wood grown in well managed forests.
The manufacturing processes conform to the environmental regulations of the country of origin

Printed in China by C & C Offset Printing Co Ltd, Shenzhen, Guangdong

1 3 5 7 9 10 8 6 4 2

The Butterfly Dance

Suzanne Barton

BLOOMSBURY

LONDON OXFORD NEW YORK NEW DELHI SYDNEY

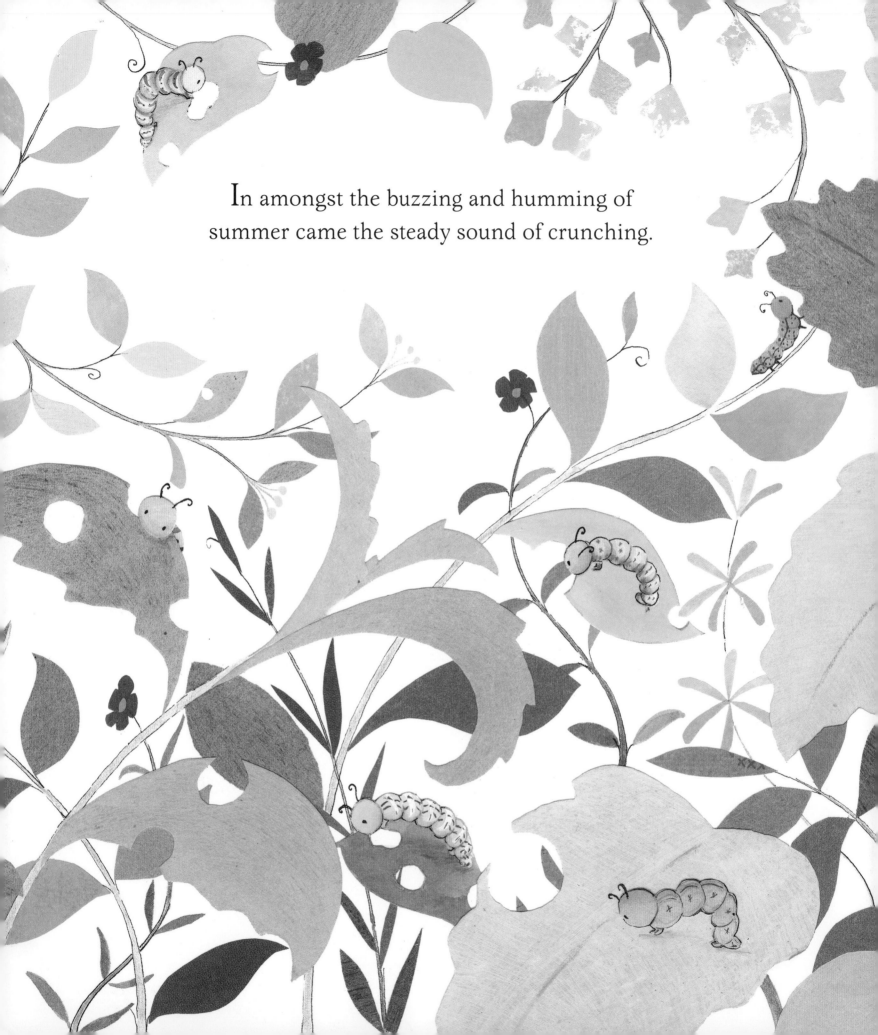

In amongst the buzzing and humming of summer came the steady sound of crunching.

Most of the caterpillars ate by themselves but
Dotty and Stripe shared everything.

One day, Stripe said,
"I'm so full, I think I'll
have a little sleep."

He spun himself a silky hammock
and snuggled up tight inside.

That's strange, thought Dotty.

"Wake up, sleepy head!"
she called. But there
was no answer.

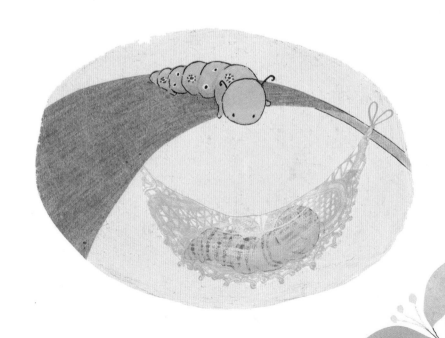

It wasn't much fun without Stripe. They'd always done everything together and Dotty felt lonely.

I'm a bit sleepy, too, she thought.

So Dotty spun herself a cosy bed and soon fell fast asleep.

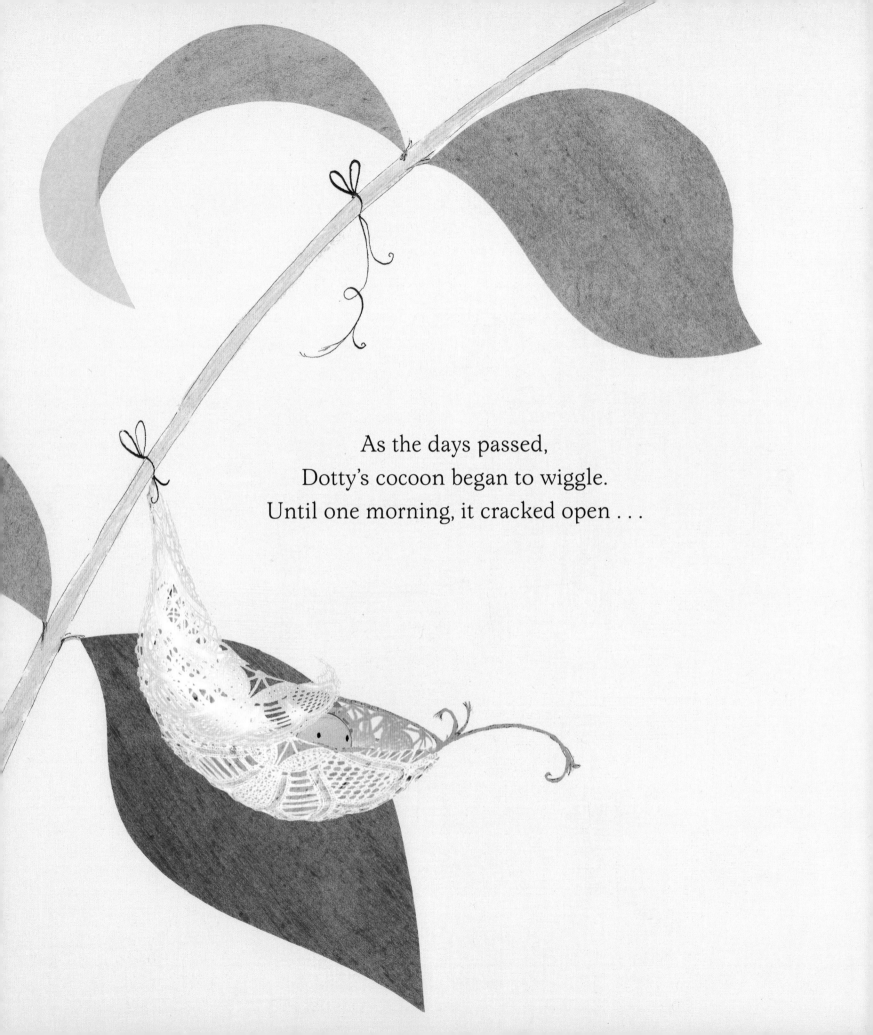

As the days passed,
Dotty's cocoon began to wiggle.
Until one morning, it cracked open . . .

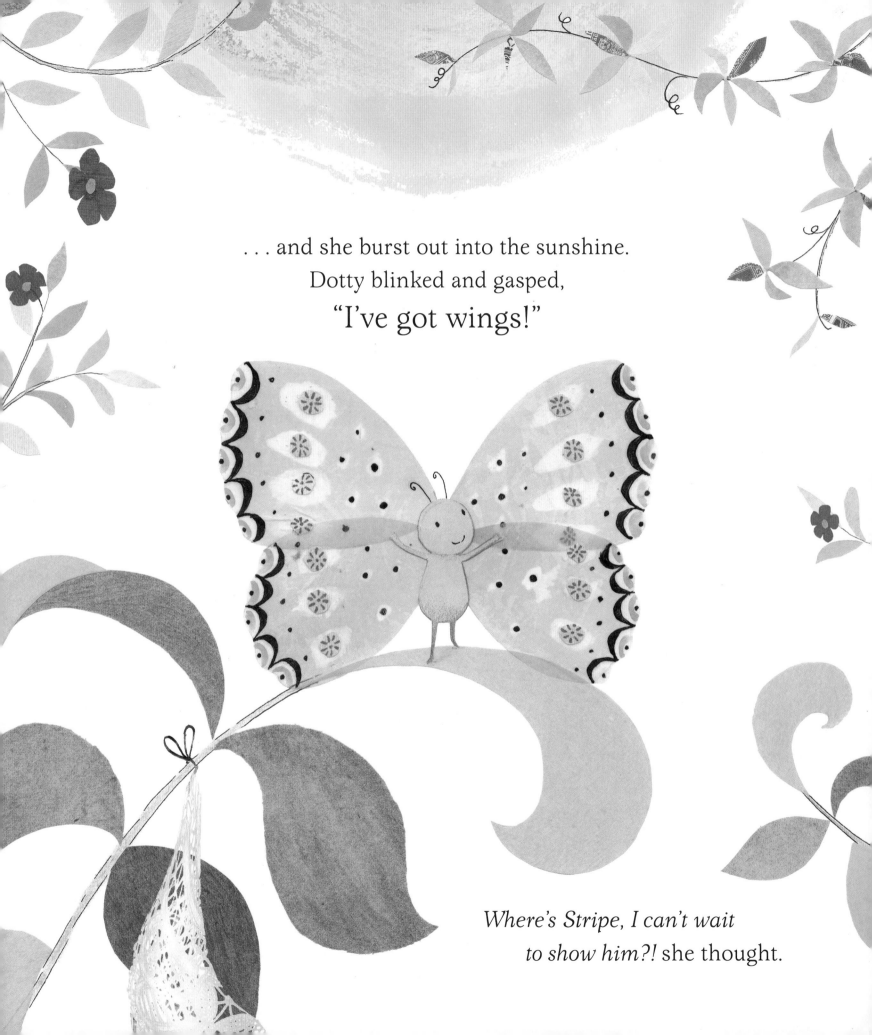

. . . and she burst out into the sunshine.
Dotty blinked and gasped,
"I've got wings!"

Where's Stripe, I can't wait
to show him?! she thought.

"Dotty!" called a dazzling butterfly gliding down beside her.

"Stripe?! Is that you?" she asked.
"Look! You've still got your stripes!"

"And you have your dots!" said Stripe.

"What shall we do now that we're
butterflies?" asked Dotty.

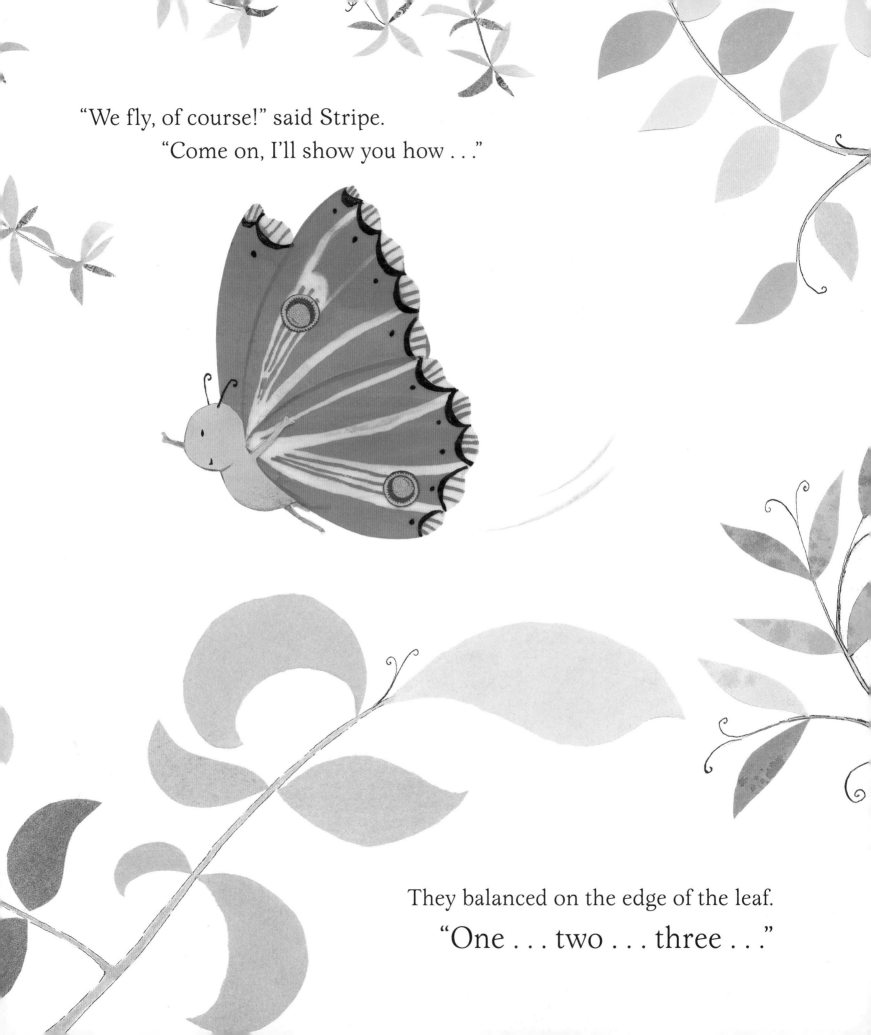

"We fly, of course!" said Stripe.
"Come on, I'll show you how . . ."

They balanced on the edge of the leaf.
"One . . . two . . . three . . ."

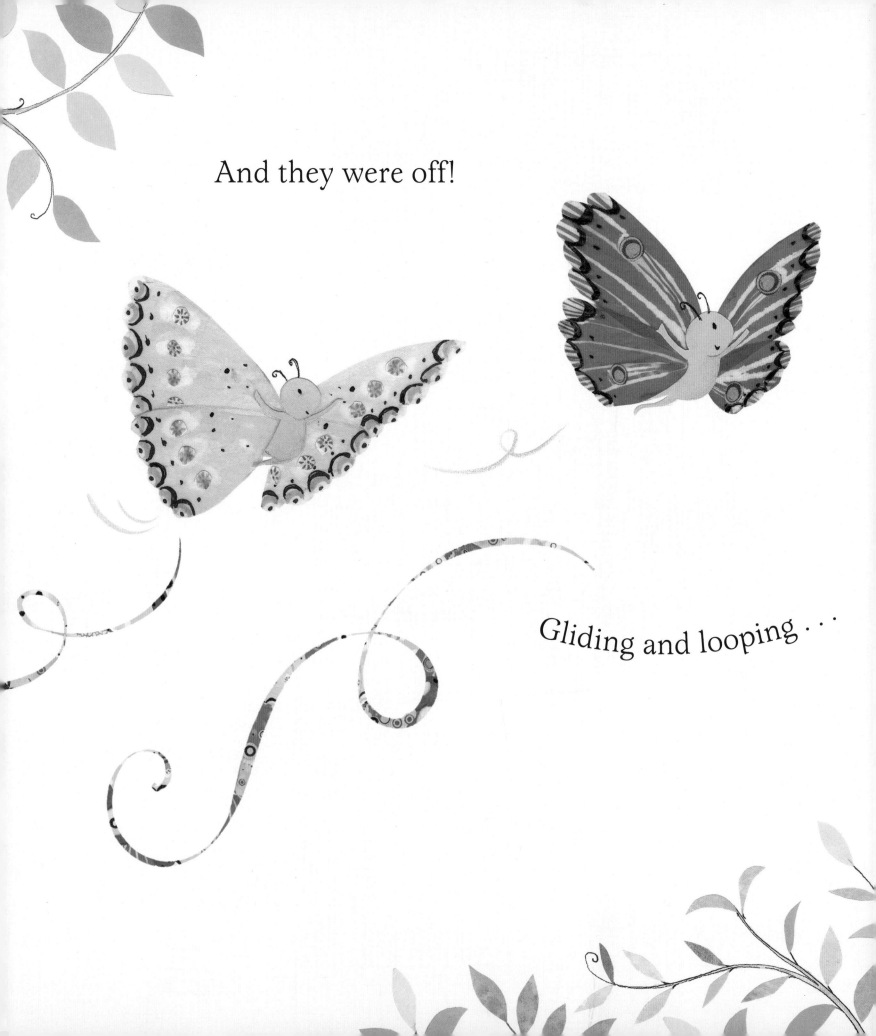

And they were off!

Gliding and looping . . .

soaring and whirling, fluttering and chasing.

Until raindrops sent
them diving for cover.

"I'm hungry," said Stripe.

A little bee popped out from a flower. "These bluebells are tasty but you might prefer the thistles."

"And you might like the poppies," another bee told Dotty.

"The meadow's full of flowers," they buzzed.

"Where's the meadow?" asked Dotty.

"Through the trees," buzzed the bees.

And as the rain stopped and the bees danced
away to make honey, Dotty and Stripe
fluttered off to the woods.

Stripe liked flying fast and Dotty liked flying high,
but best of all they liked flying together.

Far below, they saw a group of
dragonflies in a puddle.
"Let's go for a paddle," said Dotty,
and down they swooped.

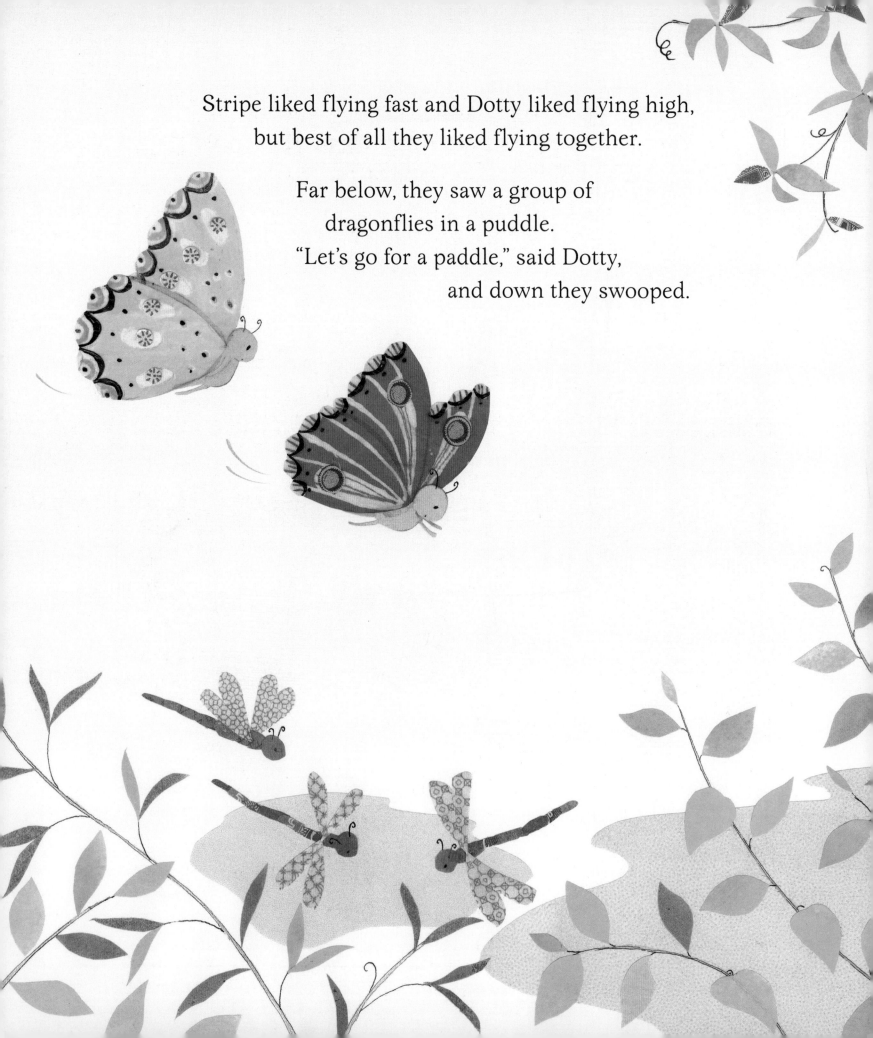

They sipped the cool water and splashed in the mud.
"Are you looking for the other red butterflies?" said
a dragonfly. "They're down by the thistles."

"Others?" said Dotty.

"Maybe there are other butterflies that look
like me. Let's find out," said Stripe.

They fluttered through the gentle breeze until they spotted some ladybirds. Dotty asked, "Have you seen any other butterflies like us?"

"Do you mean the little blue ones?" replied a friendly ladybird. "They're playing in the poppies."

"Oh!" said Dotty. "There must be some butterflies that look like me!"

"It's funny how all the ladybirds gather together,"
said Dotty. "And the dragonflies."

"And the bees," said Stripe. "Maybe I'm supposed to
play with butterflies that look like me?"

"And I'm supposed to play with the ones
that look like me?" said Dotty.

They had never been apart before – they were BEST friends.

They sat together for a long while, and then
the two friends said goodbye.

Stripe found the red butterflies
playing hide-and-seek.

"Please can I play, too?"
he asked.

He had a great time,
but he missed Dotty.

It just wasn't the same
without her.

Dotty joined the blue butterflies
dancing among the poppies.

She had fun but wished
Stripe were there, too.

"I miss my friend," Dotty said to one
of the blue butterflies. "But I can't be
with him anymore. He's with the other
red butterflies, in the thistles."

"It's only because they love the taste of
thistles!" said the butterfly. "You can
still play with your friend. Come on,
I've got something to show you . . . !"

And off they flew until they came to . . .

. . . the meadow.

"Wow!" said Dotty. "So many friends,
and they're all playing together!"

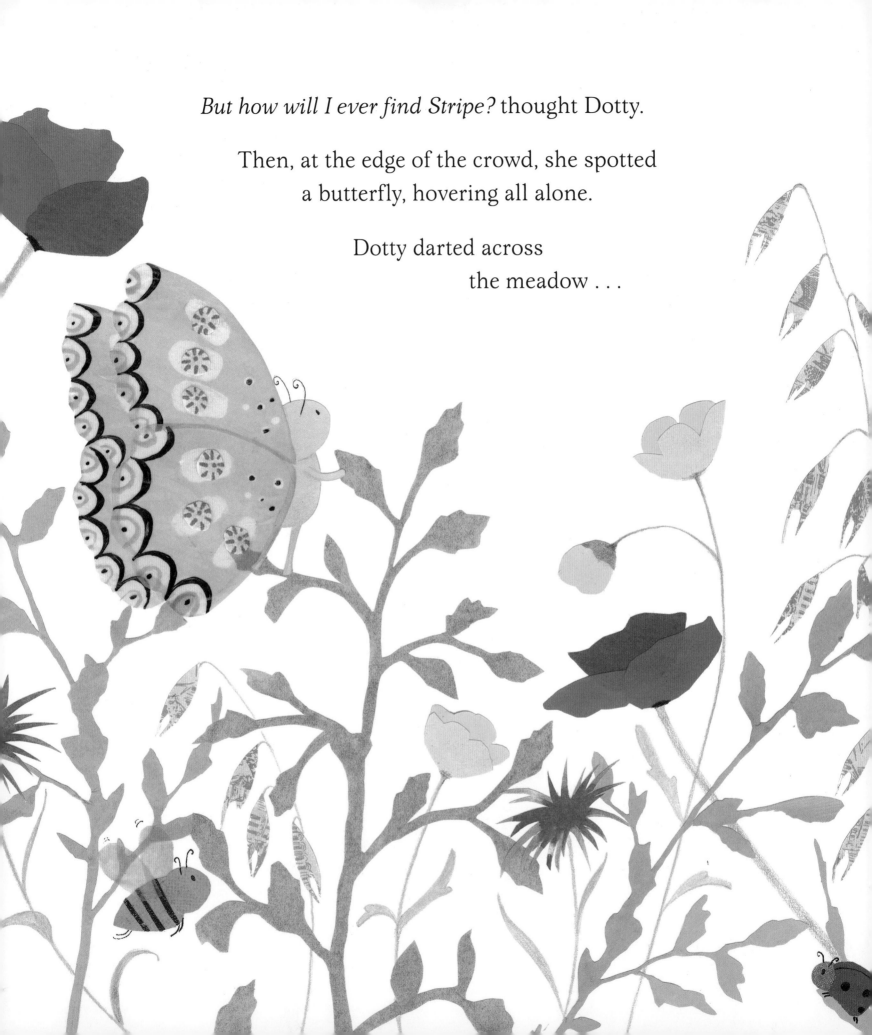

But how will I ever find Stripe? thought Dotty.

Then, at the edge of the crowd, she spotted
a butterfly, hovering all alone.

Dotty darted across
the meadow . . .

"Stripe!" she called.
"I missed you!"

"And I missed you!"
said Stripe.

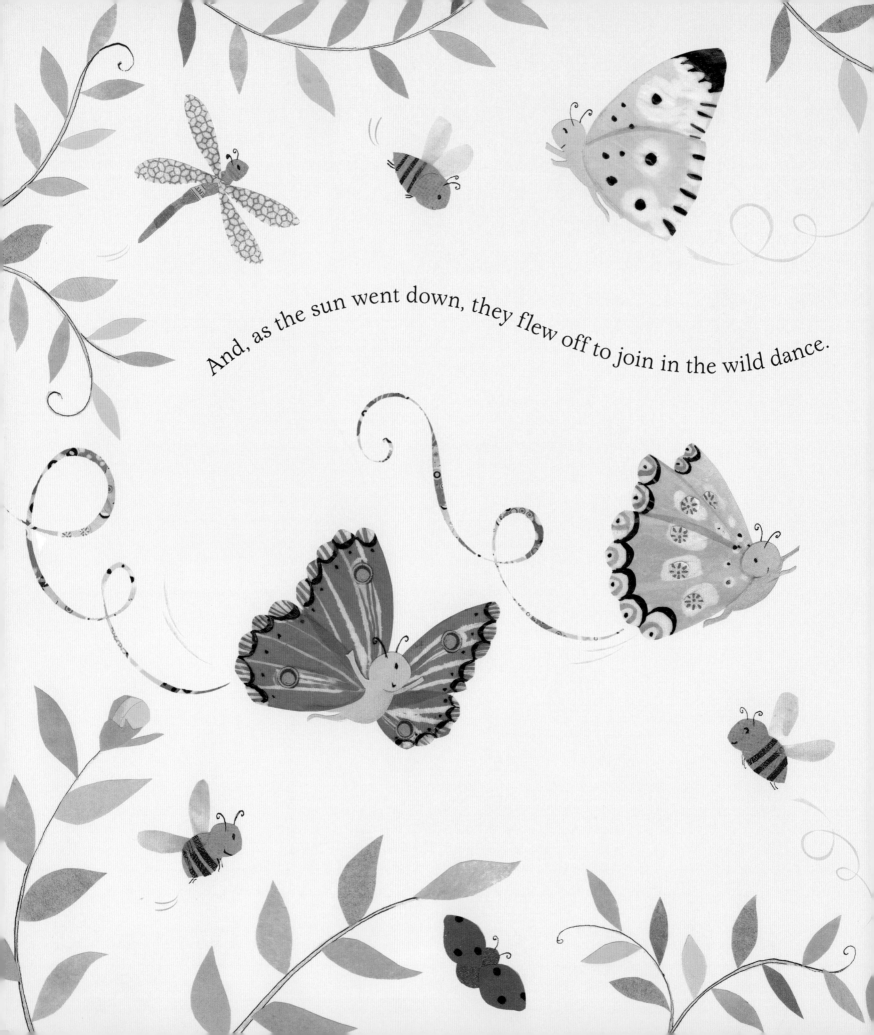

And, as the sun went down, they flew off to join in the wild dance.